T0209188

MR. "T" (Dwindal C. Tolivar)
The big man from Virginia
Big enough to see the little things
Gentle enough to express them on canvas

The Last Piece of the Pie

Born in Elkton, Virginia, 3 miles from the nearest paved road, this self-taught artist began his artistic journey with color crayons at the age of 6, when he transcribed the Greek version of the Lord's Prayer.

Having received such high praise from his grandmother, this young artist was continually inspired into cross-pollinating his creative gift from painting, to poetry, to music, while experiencing a serious flirtation with professional football and baseball somewhere in between. He also has a black belt in Judo and Karate.

After a lifetime of having circumscribed most of the creative sphere, Mr. T has ended up right where he began; with his first love, painting. Accordingly he is now devoted to nurturing that love for the remainder of his life in California

THE LAST PIECE OF THE PIE

DWINDAL C. TOLIVER

BALBOA.
PRESS

A DIVISION OF HAY HOUSE

Balboa Press books may be ordered through booksellers or by contacting:

Balboa Press
A Division of Hay House
1663 Liberty Drive
Bloomington, IN 47403
www.balboapress.com
1 (877) 407-4847

Because of the dynamic nature of the Internet, any web addresses or links contained in this book may have changed since publication and may no longer be valid. The views expressed in this work are solely those of the author and do not necessarily reflect the views of the publisher, and the publisher hereby disclaims any responsibility for them.

The author of this book does not dispense medical advice or prescribe the use of any technique as a form of treatment for physical, emotional, or medical problems without the advice of a physician, either directly or indirectly. The intent of the author is only to offer information of a general nature to help you in your quest for emotional and spiritual well-being. In the event you use any of the information in this book for yourself, which is your constitutional right, the author and the publisher assume no responsibility for your actions.

Any people depicted in stock imagery provided by Getty Images are models, and such images are being used for illustrative purposes only. Certain stock imagery © Getty Images.

Print information available on the last page.

ISBN: 978-1-9822-1246-9 (sc)
ISBN: 978-1-9822-1247-6 (e)

Balboa Press rev. date: 12/10/2018

Certificate of Registration

This Certificate issued under the seal of the Copyright
Office in accordance with title 17, *United States Code*,
attests that registration has been made for the work
identified below. The information on this certificate has
been made a part of the Copyright Office records.

Maria A. Pallante

Register of Copyrights, United States of America

Registration Number

TX 7-473-464

**Effective date of
registration:**

September 9, 2011

Title

Title of Work: The Last Peace Of The Pie

Completion/Publication

Year of Completion: 2011

Date of 1st Publication: July 29, 2011

Author

Author: Dwindal C. Toliver

Author Created: fiction

Work made for hire: No

Citizen of: United States

Year Born:

Anonymous: No   Pseudonymous: No

Copyright claimant

Copyright Claimant: Dwindal C. Toliver

125 W Beryl St R108, Redondo Beach, CA, 90277

Limitation of copyright claim

Previously registered: No

Basis of current registration: This is the first published edition of a work prev. registered as unpublished.

This is the first application submitted by this author as claimant.

Certification

Name: Dwindal C. Toliver

Date: July 29, 2011

Copyright Office notes: Regarding limitation of claim: some photographs credited to other sources.

v

CONTENTS

INTRODUCTIONS

1. The short story is about fiction. The unknown spirit. My belief,my theory, my vision and thought / paranormal, remote viewing and above all my Soul Light Dream Consciousness of Positive Energy of Reality.
2. This is a book about changes. Not physical change but a mind open to change of spirit, energy and thought into a better life of reality
3. A basic concept of one belief in a higher soul consciousness of life.
4. To make one wonder, "Could this be real or believed?"
5. A picture is worth a thousand words.
6. Follow me into the snapshot picture of a soul light consciousness of positive energy of reality.
7. Welcome the change and feel the positive energy of solitude
8. My theory is about a new beginning, a poem of life, a song of life and pictures of life.
9. My theory is an open book, right or wrong, believe it or not.

The answer to believe is an open mind to love. Do unto others as you would like to receive.

CHAPTER 1

"THE LAST PIECE OF THE PIE" THE SOUL LIGHT DREAM CONSCIOUSNESS POSITIVE ENERGY OF REALITY

Ecology says that man is not the king, despite his illusions. He must obey certain ecological rules and must heed them. Continued disregard of these laws will probably not bring extinction of life, but will bring about dissatisfaction, bewilderment and discomfort to mankind.

Today, each of us confronts the grave prospect of life in a world depleted of basic and essential resources. Open space, clean water, fresh air – each of us shoulders a personal burden: the responsibility to reverse a dramatic and destructive trend. No one can afford to be uninformed. One must go back to the basic rules and the basic concept of life and to obey the simple rules of preserving life.

What a wonderful policy that one had years ago, having an open door, open windows policies while airing out one's rooms and no security problems. But with the increasing population and greater demands for bigger and better products, we are building and producing more raw materials than ever before. The growing demand for housing, factories, cars and farming has increased tremendously over the years.

My soul-light dream consciousness, positive energy travel will bring one back into a heavenly solitude of reality.

This book is not written in the regular format. I don't want it to be, because my soul-light dream of life is like a puzzle. This puzzle is

1

introduced to mankind as an experiment. Right or wrong concept. Good and bad. All mankind should learn how to live with one another. What a wonderful basic concept. We did not learn from history and now one must make a vast turn about. We will soon be history if we continue on this present course. It is so bad that one cannot love or understand their next-door neighbor. Take a look in the mirror. Take a look into your soul light dream of reality. Do you like what you see? If yes, you are conceited. Selfish righteousness is what one has become. If one looks in the mirror and sees one's self in the image of a soul-light belief, loving all mankind, one is on the right path of soul-light dream of consciousness of positive energy of reality.

TAKE A SNAPSHOT PICTURE OF ME IN MY SOUL-LIGHT DREAM STATE AND YOU'LL SEE, MY SOUL-LIGHT CONSCIOUSNESS, ENERGY OF REALITY.

My main reason in writing this book, it's not about you. It's about me. Why? Because I am ONE person. I have one life to give. I can only live my life to the best of my abilities! I need to take control of the one and only life that I will ever have on this Earth. Why not make the best of it? The one step I can make is one of the pieces of the puzzle. I am in a soul-light consciousness energy state of mind!

Please follow me! The air that I breathe is only one Nano second of the soul-light air that you breathe, to start the wheel turning, but the energy is connecting us. So put our hands together to solve the Heavenly Body soul-light of reality problems that exist here on Old Mother Earth.

It only takes one baby step to travel in the soul-light dream into the right direction. With the brainwashing propaganda of artificial existence our life can have no time concept. One must follow the time positive energy reality of life. If my book was not in type form and you could take a look at my basic handwriting, sometimes I print, sometimes I write, and sometimes I can hardly make out my writing. I believe that the reason that I am writing this book is that my soul-light connection is helping and informing me to convey my thoughts in a soul-light manner, without a set pattern. A lot of times I have entertained the thought of stopping this book because, at times, I feel that I am not qualified to write a book without formal training or higher learning. The only thing that kept me going is that I have a direction, a conviction and an open mind of soul-light dream consciousness of positive energy of reality. No, I am not sick. Some people think that I am smoking something funny. I am writing this book because I am a lonely person. I live by myself. I am a self made man. I believe in God and I won't ask God for His help. If my book doesn't workout I have no one to blame but myself. When I talk to my friends about this book, they reply, "What have you been smoking?" I have not had a ghostwriter to help me with this book. I won't change my basic concept about my dream soul-light connection.

I see this every night in my dream state of mind. I hope that I will never lose it. My dream soul light gives me comfort and solitude. I am in touch with my soul-light beyond. I have a open avenue like never before, and I hope and pray that this book will help others to get in contact with their soul-light dream consciousness positive energy of life reality. I don't know where I got this name (soul-light). The symbol is 00 in my soul light connective to the other cycle soul light of reality. I saw it in my dream. I can shut my eyes or keep my eyes open and see the connection of two 00 soul-light entities and by seeing this I understand the soul-light connection. That is why I am writing this book.

I don't know it all, I don't want to know it all. I don't think I will cover it all. This is a simple book about what we all should see and feel. Learn how to meditate! Get away from the TV, newspapers and radio! Go to the ocean! Feel the energy from the water. Go to the mountains! Feel the energy. Go to the desert that helps us to sustain life! Feel the energy. Feel the air! Appreciate what Mother Nature/Mother Earth has provided for us! Give back to life and you have played your part in the large wheel of life. Life is like a puzzle.

In order to fulfill our part, we must all play our own part. Old Mother Earth is that big wheel of life reality. One day all of our soul-lights will be together as one wheel of soul-life, always turning for a better way of life.

I am only going to mention about the weather patterns that will change our way of life. There are other destructive forces in life that one must understand right away, but it will come in a gradual state or form. Winter, summer, spring and fall will all be one-day events. When that happens, look out for the big destruction!

The puzzle, at the present, is the way one is living with disregard for mankind's resources. Taking more and giving less. But few of the so-called wars that we've had were not in protective, save face manner. The hate derived from these wars has caused mistrust and hate throughout the land and country. The oil that one needs. The great demands will soon bring us disgrace, because greed will not accept others means of living. We are in a time zone of destruction! Sometimes power and greed will play it way out and come to a compromise. The time is now!

History has given one a good lesson to correct our future problems, but there are obstacles in the way. Hate, prejudice and greed! Why haven't we learned our lesson? United States vs. Russia, United States vs. China – what a game of warfare one is playing! There is so much distrust there, but we are still taking our main resources from other countries! When will the bubble burst? Will the weather destruction come before the bad war? We have to get in touch with our soul-light 00 consciousness energy travel into reality very soon. Please get on board with me! The puzzle can be solved!

CHAPTER 2

A SNAPSHOT PICTURE OF MY SOUL LIGHT DREAM OF CONSCIOUSNESS OF POSITIVE ENERGY OF REALITY

At first when I had my first encounter with my soul light, I did not take it seriously. I woke up from the dream with a lot of questions. I was seeing things that I thought at the time did not seem real or believable. I got up from my bed and went into the bathroom, sitting there meditating about my dream state of mind.

After returning to bed, I fell back into this deep out of body experience. Sleep.

I could see things and events like I had never seen before. I thought about my home, where I was born. I was there reminiscing about my past life. It was so real! I could see my grandmother working as a midwife, delivering babies into the world. As a young child I remember the conversations on how to take care of the baby, on preserving food and on how hard it was to make a living and, surprisingly enough, I can remember seeing my grandmother making the salmon croquettes we had every Friday. And I can make those same salmon croquettes now. As my mind kept wandering, I came in contact with my soul light dream guide and that is when I was given the wisdom to convey my thoughts and beliefs to you.

The next morning when I woke up, as I lie in bed asking myself, "did I really experience this wonderful connection of a soul light dream?"

We were like two cycle lights communicating like we had known each other for a long period of time. We talked in a positive consciousness energy experience. It was so wonderful. I did not want to wake up, but I was told I needed seven dreams to understand the 5-dimension process and how old Mother Earth will be saved.

The first dream was all about how we live in the present time here on Earth. When I was shown the snapshot picture it was sad to see the direction that this world is going in, without any hope.

The soul light dream consciousness of positive energy of reality is a stage and all soul light dream consciousness of positive energy must play its part. So, let's combine our soul light dreams and be as one!

The stage, vision, connectivity, energy, reliability, thought spirit and hope will play its part in the stage of reality.

SNAPSHOT PICTURE OF MY SOUL LIGHT DREAM #1

A small snapshot picture of the soul light consciousness energy of reality is using our Dream State of mind into a new dimension. Take only one picture and one can see a thousand ways of life in that one picture. In the Dream State, the past, present and future and the everlasting will work on the dreams of the four seasons – winter, spring, summer and fall dream concept. The basic concept is to think like a child, full of guidance but with no preconceived prejudice

A picture is worth a thousand words. Remote viewing is a tool to help one to go into a new dimension. Our future depends on telepathy and remote viewing. The new dream and the old dream will return into one soul light and mind, a conscious concept of reality. Each snapshot picture of our soul light dream will determine one further into this new basic concept of moving into the last code of life. Why a secret code? To give one a vision to build on the mystery of the solar system. The last piece of the pie is that mystery code. Our soul light conscious energy of reality. Follow me with your dreams! Take that picture that is worth a thousand words and you will enter into the soul light consciousness energy of positive reality.

SNAPSHOT PICTURE OF MY SOUL LIGHT DREAM #2

There will be a major change in the United States and other countries in reference to water, oil, gas, food and advanced technology. I am getting ahead of myself on why this will happen.

Earthquakes in Japan, Korea and China will destroy most of the area for producing food. They will depend heavily on the United States, England, Russia and France to supply food. Japan and China will be able to bounce back because of the use of Nano Technology robot programs to manufacture other resources to compete on a global status. Russia, England, Germany and France will endure an Ice Age, and with advanced Nano Technology, they will be able to produce and manufacture products with underground living and nuclear power. The United States will be hit with severe weather patterns that will also turn them to underground living, but with advanced technology, with robots and nuclear technology, they will also survive. Life style, living, will be drastic!

This is the breakdown on how humans will exist under these circumstances. My theory and belief.

There have been many books written about the Ice Age, the Melt Down Theory, The Matrix (robots vs. humans) even the code about the Bible. There have been many theories by several individuals predicting chains of events. Remote viewing is here and should not be taken lightly. I am just adding on to those predictions, theories and beliefs, not in an advanced way that one cannot comprehend, but a basic concept of belief and understanding of all of the weather destruction that is coming. My basic concept of soul light energy and consciousness reality will not take away one's strong belief in life's reality. All one must believe during this strong weather destruction period of time is this: one was put on this Earth to live and die and to pass on to everlasting life into the heavenly body of solitude.

The big change is the present lifestyle of brainwashing and forgetting about the past. Go back to the basic concept of life in general so that one can accept the New Beginning of Human Soul Light Consciousness of Positive Energy of Reality of the advanced lifestyle of living.

I will attempt to bring one's soul light consciousness of positive energy of reality into advanced way of living by telepathic communications and positive energy.

Take the present way of life one is living. Some may say it can't get any better. Some may think that it is the rich man's fault. There are so many tangible things out there that could be the problem, but there isn't time to blame our fellow man. That is all negative energy that, to be honest, could be used in a positive way of soul light energy of life reality.

My soul light consciousness of positive energy of reality is used in a positive way. There is no negative energy in one's soul light path. But in order to experience this, one must endure the four weather patterns, winter, spring, summer and fall. These patterns one is familiar with and lived under this umbrella for a long period of time. One would say, "What a beautiful way to live", and others who experience bad weather with death and destruction would have a different view. But in all there was destruction on old Mother Earth and a new beginning was formed. Even though one did not learn from the past. War, race, religion, color and greed will divide us all over again but, this time, it will be different.

SNAPSHOT PICTURE OF MY SOUL LIGHT DREAM #3

Knowledge of soul light and its related belief in all religions is the heavenly soul connection. I will introduce at the end of my book the secret to how old Mother Earth will sustain life.

A snapshot picture of my soul light dreams. Short story.

Soul light set up like the United Nations. A heavenly body of all souls represented on Earth. A good will soul light that will draw all souls together in one soul light of understanding. No race. No color. One soul telepathy for good, solitude and everlasting life.

The heavenly body is the center of soul light. The soul light will travel through a magnetic field in order to reach the Heavenly Center.

One's soul light must go through a processing center. The Black Hole Soul Travel is the secret. Where there is darkness there will be soul light and no more human darkness. Solitude is very important for soul light travel.

Humans have this ability through mind over matter. Through advanced technology (Nano Technology) this will happen to a selective few. Telepathic communication and understanding before the bad weather comes.

There is no time in soul light travel. No distance, just soul light, solitude travel. One thought and one is there into the 4, 5 and 6 dimensions.

When one dies, one's soul light enters into a Soul Light Bank. What one believed when one was a human being will determine how long one will stay in the Soul Light Bank and move on into the heavenly body or return to Earth Soul Light Center.

The soul light that communicated with me was in a dream. A dream that I had over and over again. That my soul light/brain mind travel out of my body in a dream connection to a soul light. The soul light that was introduced to me was in a form of a light, a cycle, a metamorphic form. We intertwined and communicated by telepathy. A beacon of light, like Morse Code. I was like a child with an open soul light mind. It was very easy for me to understand, with free will and no doubts.

The numerologists tell their story about the future of life here on Earth. I believe their story.

Microbiology. Bio Technology will also play a big part in this change; some say that there will be a big change in our lifestyle by using stem cell research and Nano Technology within the coming 6 to 12 years.

Quantum Physics. 4, 5, and 6 dimensions will also play a big part in the way one lives today and in the future.

Scientists with their advanced technology have advanced leaps and bounds that the normal person cannot comprehend. This technology, that's why my book is about the basic concept of life, one soul light, this is what I believe.

Plot. (Theory)

Understand the stars, earthquakes, underwater volcanoes and eruption. How to submerge under water and reappear on Earth. A new beginning.

Energy vs. The Big Wheel Concept of Reality of Life

No matter how small the dot representing one's living energy soul, we are all connected. We depend on each other to exist in this vast misunderstood world of reality.

In order for one to understand my basic concept of reality, or one concept of reality, is to believe in one reality of life. One's consciousness, spirit, soul, energy travel life through telepathy will advance human existence into the future.

Theory and beliefs. Religious beliefs, scientific beliefs, human beliefs, that one is missing the one belief that can save us all and that is the Soul, Spirit and Consciousness belief in the reality of life. The basic concept of common science connecting our human soul here on Earth to the energy soul consciousness of life. Listen to me! This can be accomplished if one will open up their minds. I believe in the soul light travel consciousness travel with energy technology. The human being state is an experience of reality. You may think you have the power here on earth, but you are the child of a greater power.

Have a Soul Light Dream! Get on board! One soul!

SNAPSHOT PICTURE OF MY SOUL LIGHT DREAM #4

My soul light explained to me in my dream that there were humans on three other planets, millions of years ago, far more advanced than any technology known today. These three planets were in competition with each other for food, water and technology in order to live. The three planets could not go to war against each other because the three planets could destroy each other with the push of a button. That is how their advanced technology kept each other in balance. But over a long period of time, weather patterns changed so vastly that the three planets needed each other's help for survival.

Food growth was non-existent, a pill was developed to take the place of food, because of the vast weather changes, no day, no night for long periods of time, their source of feeding or living on pills supplies soon dwindled. With their advanced technology, the three planets formed a union and came up with the idea to change this continuous weather of destruction pattern (there was darkness for three months at a time with no light). The sun was their only obstacle. No sun energy power.

The three planets are in a three dimensional triangle. Using their advanced technology, they set out to control the sun's energy. By trying to accomplish this fate, the three planets do not exist today. Because my soul light explained that the energy from the sun is the energy to help form a path to the 5th dimension and on Mother Earth's scientists try to use this technology because of the vast amounts of weather pattern problems, trying to control the sun's energy, they will also be destroyed.

Scientists will find a solution into the dark mater/black hole energy travel by using a 5-dimension technology. My concept, without any mathematical experience is only a theory. To understand soul light travel by using sub consciousness and consciousness spirit energy travel into the 5 dimensions. The theory - without negative energy you have to have positive energy. The new theory is that by combining negative and positive energy in the 5 dimensions, two magnetic fields, negative and positive, one can travel into the 5 dimensions by using the quantum physics technology of soul light / spirit consciousness / telepathy travel. Time travel with remote viewing, without the human body state.

If all humans are connected with energy in one shape or form, if one truly believes in my soul light dream consciousness of positive energy of life reality, this fate is possible.

SNAPSHOT PICTURE OF MY SOUL LIGHT DREAM #5.

MY SOUL LIGHT BELIEF

This will be my guideline to introducing my concept that one soul can live in one body or mind (by Nano Technology) half brain half mechanical. This future technology, man vs. technology vs. soul light travel in a mind over matter state, will help prepare the spirit (soul) when it leaves the human body.

The soul must prepare for human death to enter the soul light of solitude and travel on to a staging area of the heavenly body.

How much value one puts on one's life while living will have a direct bearing on one' soul light existence in the hereafter.

I believe that when one dreams it is a concept of one's mind in a sleep state, introducing one soul to travel in a mind concept to learn about and prepare one's soul to be introduced to the wonders of the soul light heavenly body.

How does soul light communicate?

Telepathic. Two soul lights as one, with an open soul light understanding (soul light is good, positive energy). Thinking that this concept is so vivid and so basic a concept that one soul light, one human being, should have one direction to go in a positive soul light dream consciousness of reality.

Advanced Nano Technology, a chip put in the brain, will be able to go on line CP and read data in an advanced state of mind.If one human being believes in the Bible and follows it, understanding that by believing in God after death there is a place for one in Heaven. One God – one concept to believe in and follow, without proof is unbelievable blind faith, but it's the best as one lives now and exists into the future. With Nano Technology using brain function as half bio human function and half Nano (chip) function, one's soul can leave the body to carry out different tasks in preparing one's soul to exsiccate, leave one's body after death. All one's soul needs is just one soul light connection to communicate – telepathic light. This one soul light is so knowledgeable about what the future holds and after for old / new Mother Earth. My Soul Light Dream introduced me to this faith. That is why I am writing this book, The Last Piece of the Pie. This concept may change as I continue writing this book, but, as of now, I cannot think of a better concept to introduce the soul that lives temporarily within one's body and will depart one's human body upon death and enter into the soul light consciousness of reality

Believing that upon death one's soul will live forever in the kingdom of heaven, where no human being has seen, just believes. What a beautiful concept, and I believe this concept. I truly believe that the inner soul has a direct relation and knowledge of the present way of life here on Earth and hereafter (human soul consciousness vs. soul light energy travel). There will be a drastic change in how human beings communicate here on Earth, mainly because of advanced Nano Technology (humans vs. mechanical – robots). I will talk about this further in my book, but only in a past or future way of life reality.

When one takes a picture in one location after another, one uses these pictures for future reference.

My Snapshot Pictures of Soul Light Dream of Consciousness energy of Realty book operates on this theory. When one reads my snapshot vision of events, take a good look at that thought vision picture with an open mind and compassionate understanding. Sometimes one has to review the snapshot vision to understand the plot that will come on a Snapshot Picture of a Soul Light Dream of Consciousness Energy of Reality. Part of the plot is in the start, middle and the end. Don't get discouraged. Have an open mind! Be a part of my soul light dream!

This concept has lasted from the days BC up to the present. Wars have been fought over religious beliefs and the concept is still strong.

If one can believe that mankind has a living soul within one's body, where is this soul that lives in one's body?

My concept is that the soul comes in a form of a Nano Technology that exists in one's brain. Even the Nano Technology concept of putting a chip into the brain to store information will work, but what is missing is the soul light dream consciousness of positive energy of reality to enter into the 4, 5 and 6 dimension and on to eternity.

SNAPSHOT PICTURE OF MY SOUL LIGHT DREAM #6

My Snapshot Picture of Soul Light Consciousness Energy of Reality

The soul light is in the shape or form of a soul light heavenly body consciousness of energy of reality of a round cycle, one point to the other, is absolute light that travels into the 5 dimensions using a magnetic field for stability and direction. One thought, one mind, one energy soul travel. One is there.

Communication (soul light) 4 to 5 dimension is telepathic with light movements or on/off codes of travel.

One soul light communicating with another soul light for travel and knowledge. The concept is only two soul lights need to be connected, store their knowledge, can leave an open channel through 4 and 5 dimensions and have a round table communication with other interested soul light parties.

Soul light communication – Intertwine soul light on/off in 4 to 5 dimensions talking with each other.

The Bible followers believe that there is one God in the hereafter. God is a spirit, a soul with no physical features. God could be a man or a woman. A billion plus people have believed this concept since the beginning of time. The Koran, Buddhism, etc – there has to be a way to communicate. (Why not soul light communication through the telepathic 4 and 5 dimensions?)

Soul Spirit. An alien is in my soul light dream. I am using these two soul lights communicating with each other with the understanding that using Nano Technology could be in the form of a billion 4 to 5 dimension concept of communicating with the Soul Light Angel.

All soul light communication has no secret. Soul light knowledge is an open book. Their main function is to help new or old soul lights in the direction of the heavenly body so when I used the term "soul light concept of two soul lights (energy on/off) communicating with constant consciousness/energy flow', physical energy is there in the past, the present and the future. The soul light located in the brain does not have any direct bearing on the human being, other than when one has one's own belief, an open channel is open to a feeling of warmth and serenity. Keep that faith into soul light heaven.

A small soul light, 0 Nano size, stays at that size upon leaving the body and becomes a baby soul light that is seeking soul light knowledge and growth. One has to be reborn. The same principle as one is born into life on Earth but the process is far more advanced and sophisticated. Before I die I will have been able to communicate with soul light in my dream state of mind. By communicating by telepathic means I have been given the knowledge of what will happen to old Mother Earth in the near future. This is not an exact science but a wakeup call for the future of old Mother Earth's existence. This is my soul light dream theory about Mother Earth's longevity and major changes in how one will be living now and in the future.

The Future. From the soul light Nano Technology, I believe in the soul / spirit alien technology into the 4 to 5 dimensions.

The big test to enter in the soul light consciousness of positive energy of reality is that one must have the knowledge to perform remote viewing and be put in a dream state of reality of their own free will. These dreams will give you the secret.

SNAPSHOT PICTURE OF MY SOUL LIGHT DREAM #7

Everyone will be given a dream soul light test. Seven dreams will be given to test one's free will and beliefs. Humans all over the world (Mother Earth). One reaction from this test is that where everyone lives one will be tested with unbelievable disasters that will determine whether one human soul light will travel into this stage of suspended elevation and solitude and remain until Earth is ready for one to return. The other destruction will come as fast as lightning, vanishing like a flash of lightning in a form like the Bermuda Triangle or a black hole. No destruction of Mother Earth. Only the human beings will disappear vanish mysteriously. The reason why this will come about is the fifth dimension of the 12 pyramid war. The code will be revealed. The sun, sol, is the vehicle used for soul light energy reality to enter the soul heavenly body. The highest intelligence of human beings did not go along with the rule of law.

There will be three stages of destruction the human beings will be able to survive.

Ice Age. The body will be frozen in a pneumatic sleep trance with the Nano chip in the brain, working with robots and machines. One will be able to sustain life for three years with the aid of Nano Technology. The machines and robots will be made of iceberg figures, everything operating in a frozen mode. All movement will be made in a telepathic communication with no moving parts. The energy from the cold will stimulate the parts that need to move with a drop of water as an air bubble. As the temperature gets warmer over a long period of time so will the function of the robots and machines and the frozen human beings will be able to function again. It will be like a flower opening up by the sun's rays. Humans will sustain life again but will have problems with the machines and the robots. They will think that they are the masters and will dictate how human beings will function. But as human beings get stronger and, with advanced technology that the machines and the robots did not know about, a code will be set up because of the experiences of outer space living. This code, a spider chip imbedded in the machines, the humans will be able to shut down the machines and robots at will.

PLEDGE QUESTIONS

(Before you learn the Pledge answer the questions below)

1. Can you stop and listen? Can you feel your heart beat? When it stops, can you go on into the soul light dream communicating with other energy beings?
2. Can you feel the positive energy within?
3. Are you in that dream state of openness, consciousness of positive energy of reality?
4. If so, you are entering your soul dream, your spirit and your subconscious. Pass your soul light dream to others to carry out the mission of peace.
5. If so, you are ready to take the pledge for the dream state of meeting the soul light consciousness energy of reality of life.
6. When taking the pledge, we become leaders, not followers.

THE SOUL LIGHT PLEDGE OF CONSCIOUSNESS OF POSITIVE ENERGY, VISION, SPIRIT, THOUGHT AND REALITY

THE PLEDGE

One's soul light positive energy must excel in life with maturity. One must base his or her judgment on the big picture. The advanced soul light positive energy must accomplish one, two or three positive thoughts. May not be enough. It means being able to carry out one spiritual vision and dream for a positive life of reality.

We are but a little cog in a wheel, existing in this big wheel of life. We must have the capacity to face unpleasantness, frustration, negativity, and discomfort without looking back but forward with conviction and solitude of a reality of soul light thought of life.

The soul light of positive energy means taking responsibility for one's own life. Dependability equates with personal integrity.

My pledge is to harness my positive abilities and soul light energies and to do more than is expected of me.

I'd rather aim my soul light energies high and miss the mark than to aim low and make it.

OUR GOVERNMENT AT WORK
FOLLOW THE MONEY AND
ONE WORLD ORDER.

Saddam Hussein

CHAPTER 3

OUR GOVERNMENT AT WORK

I don't want to talk bad about our government. It is the best government of all other forms of governments. I would not like to live in any other place than the United States. But we have problems that need to be addressed. For the people, of the people and by the people has lost its value.

We are a young nation compared to other nations. We need more maturity. Our government must follow the soul light dream consciousness positive energy of reality. It's time (the Big Deal). The vast amount of money in campaigning must stop. The big secret plot is coming. Look out for the women. Its time.

A snapshot picture of my soul light is worth a thousand words.

In the universe, there have been many tests and theories about how the universe functions. Man on the moon accomplished what? With our government (secret) Pathfinder landed on Mars. What have we accomplished? Ask our shadow government (secret).

I think it is safer to say that 55% of people living on Earth have a limited amount of knowledge regarding what is going on in this country, or in the world. In a way, it is not their fault. Using fear tactics, being informed about security, politics, health, religion, etc. is left up to the leaders or representatives of each state. To keep one informed about national security, with the daily activities, workload vs. manpower, keeps one in a constant state of confusion. Uninformed T.V., radio and newspapers are all biased and one seems to get brainwashed by accepting the two party system used to keep us apart with fear and no organizational strategy. One must go back to the basic concept of learning – reading, writing, math, and community values give one more of one's self, family comes first, and most of all, think of one's own belief. Do not compete with the Jones's. Compete with one's self. Don't put monetary values before self-worth. Take what one has and make the best of any situation. Above all, believe in something. Believing in hope, love and a strong conviction of one's self will lead to a happy person and a life in the soul light hereafter.

One is in the big wheel cycle of life with no ending - no solution, in sight. Work hard and be a good citizen and our government will take care of you by outsourcing jobs into other countries.

The beauty of our country is taken for granted! Even with the terrible disasters that confront us each year. We seem to overcome those obstacles and bounce back with pride. The big wheel is broken up into three (3) sections.

The little cog in the big wheel is constantly pushing for advanced opportunities with little or no resources. A tremendous drive to get ahead with sometimes-hopeless results. With so many help programs one would think,

"What more does one need to get away from the poor environment?" Some think that two years in the military would make a big difference, with strict discipline. Gangs are an escapable past. Gangs are there because of no family background. There is a solution but one has moved on to the second wheel of control. Stabilized up to a point, but holding on for dear life. Working hard to maintain one way of life is a far greater obstacle than one can manage. After ten or twenty years of hard work and reaching that retirement age, things seem to fall apart. Mortgaging our homes to stay afloat, being brainwashed by the two party system, depending on them to bail one out, failing to look at the big picture.

One's health is deteriorating because of stress, eating out too much, to satisfy the feelings of pressure. I am writing this because it has been told over and over again and again, but one doesn't know how to take a step back, go back to the basic concept of reality, and share with one another. Give to receive is long forgotten. Now here comes the Big Wheel. Only five percent of the population is in control of all aspects of government. One will ask one's self, "How can this be?" You should be part of the big wheel cycle of life. You have been brainwashed. Slowly but surely, with a false concept of reality. It looks good on the outside, but one fails to <u>follow the</u>

<u>money</u>. All kinds of promises were made but broken and you fought back brilliantly, but one has been separated by the two party system – greed.

The big wheel concept will be slowed down considerably with the third party entering the picture. The third party will be so strong that the two party system will have to combine forces. That is when the One World Order will come into existence. This will be big! There will be destruction between the second and the first wheel, fighting for what little power is left. This destruction (chaos) will happen in all of the other countries, mainly Russia, England, France and Germany. The One World Order has been in the making for some time, forming a united front of the five percent, the United States, Russia and the other power monopoly countries. Money, greed and power.

The Blue Caps will be put in place in all of these countries for the sole purpose of controlling all of the massive people out of control first and second wheel of reality. Marshall law will take effect. One of the reasons why this One World Order will be made will be the fear of China taking over the world. A threat to our One World Order way of life. Listen! One must stay and fight to maintain our way of life! What a concept, and believe it or not, one will go along with this plan! Oh yes, Mexico will be our 51st state while this is going on. Before the war breaks out. This is inevitable. It is past due. The vast changes in the weather. All countries, including the United States, will suffer the loss of millions of people. Hard rains for forty days and forty nights will surpass floods like one has never seen. The bad weather will happen slowly, over a long period of time.

My Theory goes back into history. North and South fighting at war with each other over a law, right or wrong. Millions of people perished. Has one learned one's lesson? Republicans and Democrats fight for the people. "We know what's best for you and this country!" We are the people. We have the right to vote, to demand our right to vote. But when there are disagreements, major disagreements, one must vote. The problem is that one is brainwashed by the two party system. It's wintertime. The cold war is over. What did one achieve? One is still faced with not one different belief or ideology. Is there hope? The cold war was a tough one. Many a lesson to look back and learn from. But the winter has opened a new direction of war. The cold war all over again but on a smaller scale.

The star wars version of the cold war was successful and luck was also a factor. The bottom line, what is left from the cold war, is waste material so great that we do not understand how to cope with it. Our environment is slowly disintegrating. Waste material is getting out of control and ignored. Ask one's self when it is best to fight a war? Some will say wintertime. Wintertime can give one time to regroup and think   about the future. My soul light consciousness energy of reality is asking one to stop and think! It is time for hope in the wintertime state of reality. One must be prepared for the worst. Continue to keep the eye on the storm. The code, the puzzle is coming. Question: Will the secret code stop this big wheel concept?

Plot is out there but only the soul light knows why.

This is the last (third) secret. The nuclear weapon supplied by China came from an unknown source. Because of greed and money, the C.I.A. on the wrong side (hating the United States), sold these weapons on the black market. Homeland Security will let the weapons slip into the United States when the time comes. An order will be given to destroy the United Stapes's vital strategic area point. But the terrorists will not know. When the order is given, a top spokesman for the terrorists will be telling the United States, bragging, showing their power, saying, "It's your time to suffer! Die you imperialist, capitalists!" on the air in their country. But little do they know that the nuclear weapons were a secret plan, to bring out the top terrorist leader, conducted by the United Kingdom and the United States through a third world country. The nuclear secret weapon will malfunction. The top leader in charge of the terrorists will have given away their secret location and they will be destroyed. The terrorist that came into the United States was an undercover agent (our C.I.A.).

THE BIG CONTROL FACTOR

The arms race will stop us from destroying old Mother Earth. The last big secret. Aliens will give us free energy to run our country. Money, oil, gas. Follow the money/big business/money.

Big companies/money = control vs. credibility

Problem solved! Free energy!

- Our government
- Oil
- Credibility
- Stock Market vs. Main Stream America
- Follow the Money
- Our Federal Reserve

Take a Snapshot Picture of my Soul Light Dream Theory

Fear that the third party will have to live under the One World Order rule/concept. First class, with power and direction, will brainwash masses of people through Nano Technology and the fear that one will not be able to function or exist without this. The normal day-to-day existence (work, food, medical) will be controlled by Nano Technology. For a short period of time there will be a third party. It will end. But with the two party concept you will be rich (15%) or poor (85%). One World Order will take over consisting of Russia, England, France, Germany and the United States. The above countries will control other under developed countries. The One World Order with the help of the Trilateral Commission will control water, oil, gas and precious minerals.

Our advanced technology will make these weather changes come sooner than later. Reason? To save mankind. Research will have one believe that the human body cannot exist unless one adapts to these changes (fear, Nano Technology). Alternative medicine will make a brave push for changes for human health but to no avail. Because of power and fear the stronger get stronger and the weak get weaker. That's the story of life. The Big Change is coming. The Code, the puzzle and the happy ending.

The third party snapshot picture of a party, trying to bring out the truth to the party will be ripped apart by the two party system because they have long been guilty of deception. Picture this: A third party attempting to get to the people for a change in how our government should be run. "Of the People, By the People and for the People." Green Peace, saving our economy, global warming. Picture trying to bring this important information out to the people but it cannot be accomplished because of the lack of money. Yes, Money! The root of all evil. Our shadow government will not let one follow the money! It is set up to deceive one, with oh so many deceptions. It may come to a point of deception, having a race war to solve our problems. When this happens the One World Order will take control. Take a snapshot picture of this. If this comes to pass most of your rights will be taken away. There will be no more middle class. The middle class will be destroyed.

Picture in your mind the radio of free information. In order for this radio station to remain on the air, the radio station needs sponsorship money. Follow the money. Stations need ratings and sponsorship. One needs an angle, not the true story in full, but sensationalism with an angle to make one believe that whatever one's angle is, twist the truth, sensationalism, high power thought process if the truth of reality at that time with money and advertising we'll make our radio station successful. Only in America. All other news companies follow the same principle. T.V., newspapers, etc.

One World Order controlling one with a chip implanted into one's brain as a control devise, to follow the masters that will take over mankind. One must believe in a religious faith and follow this path faithfully in order to go in the spiritual direction and excel in life's reality. Those who do not have this chip implanted into their brain, who refuse to have this chip implanted into their body, will be cast out as an outsider. That is when the two party system will have their problems. One World Order.

1. The Nano Advanced Chip party (the Plot Control Factor)
2. The Non-Nano Chip Party
3. The side effect of the Nano Chip is that it will force one to one's knees with side effects and one will depend on this Nano Chip Technology forever.

(A Snapshot Picture of my Soul Light Dream

Theory vs. Reality)

Preparation – rules to go by and understand. This is very important. One cannot attempt to express the seriousness of being prepared for the future chain of events and life style, as one knows it now

There has been talk about the tenth planet, three times larger than Earth. It has been written that millions of years ago a tenth planet came close to Earth and offset the balance of it. That is why the Earth was destroyed (believe it or not). Why not prepare for the worst destruction? 2012 will be our biggest weather change. My belief, what I heard, and its in the book. If this book doesn't do anything else but wake up one's consciousness to be prepared, and maybe you can write a book about your belief and soul consciousness. One needs the energy connection. One must see their own signs, one has been warned many times overlooked what is in front of you on a daily basis. The only reason that I can see that one does not see these warnings is because one has been brainwashed. Our daily activities are so demanding that one cannot see the forest for the trees.

The spin bits of information that one gets from the news media, T.V., Radio, is in a way of centralizing information or ideas and selling advertising and goods. Follow the money and you will see. It is big business. Brainwashed, one will not get the big picture because of this method. There is good information out there but with the one sided news media it will not get the true information, but only part of the information because of money. A little knowledge is a dangerous thing. If one doesn't get the big, full picture, one will fall in line with the massive number of people, uninformed.

We are followers. If one must follow anything, follow our soul light consciousness. Believe; go back to the basic concept of reality of life. If one can accomplish this, one will have a basic guideline to move forward in the right direction of reality and one can face the tremendous challenges of life. Life is so simple but one complicates it by worldly, religious and discontent issues. When one loves their fellow man, "do unto others and one would have them do unto you", charity and brotherhood are tools needed to have a simple life of reality. We are living in a code environment. The need to know your security reasons, one is not or will not understand the future outcome. One has been programmed to live a certain way. Our two party system dictates how one lives. One is either right or left. Compare this with the negative/positive theory. If one follows these concepts, one lives in a controlled environment. Depending on this concept, pushing one far away from what reality is all about.

Fight for a third party concept! If not, one will be living in the one world order way of life. A disabled ship. Money and power. 5% under the umbrella of control of power. (Follow the money.)

Third party concept can bring out the hidden facts that our two party system has been hiding for centuries.

One should not have to live in a two-stage party of life. One has been controlled by the two party system solely because of fear and confusion. The third party system can also show one that there are other living creatures around us, helping more than destroying our way of life. New technology is great but it is getting out of hand and will be controlled by the power/manipulation hungry (one world order) klan. One will be like zombies, existing only for amusement's sake if the One World Order takes control of our lives.

The book, The Ugly American, will soon exist again. Race, power, oil, food – will bring on the third world war or see the code. The New World Order will not let another country control the energy source of life, meaning this world. Other countries don't know that Russia and the United States are playing bad cop/good cop to keep underdeveloped countries fighting against each other with no organizational concept of the big picture. The advanced technology shared by Russia and the United States about outer space technology will control the other countries, an outer spaceman, water, food and oil are the main goal of superiority.

Follow the money. A bouncing ball will lead one to the actions and reactions. Follow the money is the key to our lifestyle. If one cannot follow the money, one is lost. Greed is one big problem, not only in this country but also in China. Greed will trickle down into their own countrymen and will be used to destroy our country from within (and also to destroy their country from within?). The human element is overlooked. A change in policy must come.

Global warming – Survival (environment) Africa is a great concept, but will stop short of the mark because of the corruption of power at the top. A big change is coming.

Helping other countries with millions of dollars in aid is only putting a band-aid on that country's problems, which are lost to aid and a movement to other unknown viruses.

United States in Iraq and Afghanistan will be involved for a long period of time. It's all about the oil. One must solve the terrorism problems by going back to where we came from. Oil in the United States was a big event at one time but a cap was put on the oil supplies for future emergencies. Underdeveloped countries with oil need expert technology. This is where greed enters the picture.

Control either with help or control taken by force equals terrorism. When will we ever learn Good vs. evil – or special interest groups with money taking advantage of the two party system, Republican vs. Democrat, Bad vs. Good. The big problem is the need to know concept. A little knowledge is a dangerous thing. One has surpassed the concept with greed and fear.

Location – Take a look at Israel, surrounded by the terrorists. To destroy Israel has been their goal for years but no action has been taken. Why? Follow the money. Follow one's belief. The politics of the United States is uncertain at this time. Looks good on the surface but look out for deception. It is a form of brainwashing. React with war is our practice or control. War, false economy for the next 10 years is good for the few, not the masses. One needs to pinpoint the terrorist soon or there will be a situation so deep in fear tactic that we will go in the direction of destroying our way of life.

Two senators were having lunch together. One senator was a Republican from Texas and the other senator was a Democrat from California. The senator from Texas commented, "You know Bob, we have known each other for almost 20 years and our politics are not that far apart." Bill told Bob (the senator from California) "I had a dream last night that you and I were running for President. Our platforms were very unique. We both won the Presidency. Bob, you would be president for four years and I would be the vice president. After four years I would be the president and you would be the vice president."

Bob (the senator from California) replied, "I had the same dream. What a brilliant concept. During those eight years we got a lot accomplished with the border problems we had. The large amount of illegal aliens in our states, Texas and California, and Arizona had gotten out of control. We both proposed a bill that Mexico becomes the fifty-first state and it passed. Brilliant!"

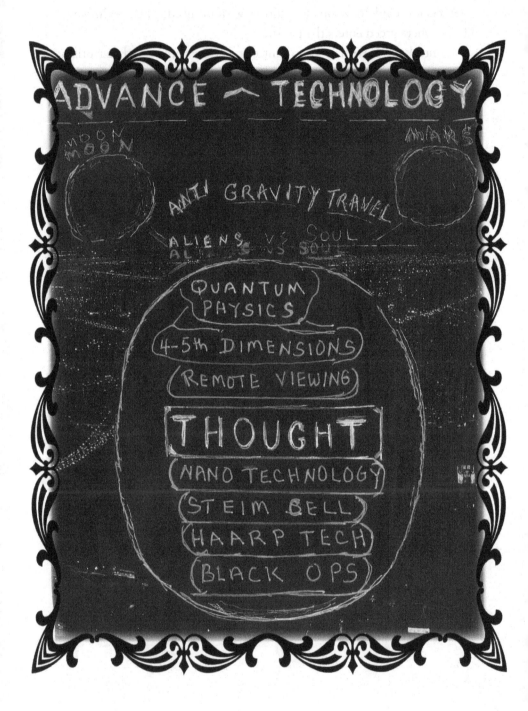

CHAPTER 4

ADVANCED TECHNOLOGY

Tools to open the door into the 5th Dimension

TOOLS: PARANORMAL TRAVEL

- Reverse Engineering
- BlakHole
- Wormhole
- TimeTravel
- My Theory to travel into the 5th Dimension is the mind over matter – subconscious and conscious in my Soul Light Dream
- Positive Energy of Reality

The Big change – the Big ending – the Big <u>thought</u> my vision- the Big build-up. Astro travel out of one's physical body – one can travel into another dimension with my soul light dream consciousness of positive energy operating in a thought spiritual movement

<u>Travel</u>: Into the unknown astro plain of the heavenly body. One must be able to complete the human free will cycle of life on Earth, believing that there is a soul light dream consciousness of positive energy of life reality.

THE ADVANCED TECHNOLOGY LIST
WITHOUT COMMENTS:

- Put your mind in a dream state
- Take each subject as if you were part of it's reality
- If one can accomplish this – one is in the advanced technology state of mind traveling into my soul light dream consciousness of positive energy of reality

My Theory (Advanced Technology) (Plot)

There are no true directions or guidelines to follow in writing my theory. The unknown is a mystery. The thought process is all based on belief. Theory and soul light dream consciousness.

Advanced Technology List (Continued)

The String Theory

1. Black OPS – Military (secret)
2. The Philadelphia Experiment – The Bermuda Triangle (History)
3. Teleporting a person vs. soul travel. Need DNA solution and soul energy soul light travel (Example – One present thought emerges, transport by positive energy consciousness a million miles away (communicated) – (my theory)
4. Star wars - big in the near future but lost on Nano Tech
5. Remote viewing and Telepath – Paranormal unnatural means – relating to my soul light dream consciousness of positive energy and reality

Big problem - why depend on what color the machines are, what nationality one robot is. Using the same concept as race as we see it on Earth. Machines will have wars with each other because of color and manufacturing countries. Why? Because of human life style – who are the best? Example: Red robot machines vs. Blue robot machines. Which one has the most destructive power? Information? Who needs it most? Many variables. Leads to war.

1. Stem cell revolution (Genetic Engineering)
2. Man living underwater (Nano Tech)
3. Half man/half machine (time travel)
4. To die means rebirth into a soul light cycle of travel (telepathic knowledge - paranormal means)
5. The human being that doesn't accept the Nano chip in one's body will be lost, will not fit into main society – outcast (out in a zoo for higher beings to enjoy)

My Snapshot Picture of Soul Light Consciousness of Energy of Reality Nano Tech will change our way of life, but be prepared – get into the main cycle of soul light of life or be lost in the outer cycle of life. (The Code vs. Nano Tech)

It's Curtain Time

If one wants to excel in life, one should learn to accomplish more than one thing in life. Accomplishing one, two or three things may not be enough. When one can fall back on one's failures and carry on with another dream and hope, one will be successful in life. Our soul light dreams are there to give us the guidance. You are a little cog in a wheel, existing in this big wheel of life. Who started the wheel to move is not important. One must get on board, go with the flow, improving each challenge and don't stop moving in the right direction of success.

Sometimes humor is very important to introduce us to the subject matter. Laughter is one of the main ingredients for a healthy life. I got off the topic to introduce a little humor. Now back to reality.

Advanced Technology on Quantum Physics travel, Quantum telepathy, electric quantum physics energy, quantum physics 4 to 5 dimension, quantum Nano technology, stem cell quantum physics. Physics is the future of our changing world. Of life, one must learn and understand dark matter, black hole, worm hole theory. Without this knowledge science will be at a standstill for future advancement into the world of the unknown.

Attum, platomum, nuetrum should be put in layman's terms. The basic concepts, so that the learning people will be able to keep up.

My Soul Light Dream Information

Accept the fact that soul/spirit aliens are living here on Earth in the form of human beings communicating with each other through telepathic means. These aliens are here to help promote and save Old Mother Earth. Could it be too late?

Why? Because of greed the One World Order is coming, controlling the water, oil, and food. Positive energy must be put in the right perspective. All religions must learn how to live in harmony. Greed that is in our health providers must stop. Alternative medicine should be on board, and put on board with other leading medical advancements. Nano Tech will have a direct bearing on how one will live in the future.

CHAPTER 5

THE BLACK HOLE

With mechanical robots and advanced technology. Why I keep harping on the basic concept is to know and to feel this basic concept of learning without advanced thinking. It's there because when one travels into 4 to 5 dimensions without one understanding of the basic concept of life, one will be lost in the 4 to 5 dimension reality.

My theory about the black matter/white matter, black hole/worm hole is very simple, as is all that is unknown. So something that is unknown, one will not take a chance to find out the unknown reality of life travel. 4 to 5 dimension travel, one human does not have to go into the black hole physically but by using mind over matter concept, one can make it's own black hole/white hole magnetic field. Example: use what one has been using for centuries to advance our way of life.

- Thought
- Vision
- Wisdom
- Creativity
- And above all – soul light dream consciousness of positive energy advanced travel of reality

Energy Travel Theory

Dark matter and white matter will have to be introduced to hold an object with magnetic field control together. If one Nano Tech light object

38

form, traveling in a Nano second, goes into 4 or 5 dimension = black hole/white hole travel. Example: Nano Tech Energy traveling in a circular motion = high volume of musical sound to form an echo. Reverse energy with white matter/dark matter = magnetic field creating a sound into white matter. There is no start/no end – movement.

Scientists with this data can expand outwardly in the 4 to 5 dimension theory. Question: The unknown – If there were people living on another planet trying to get to Earth, what would be the obstacles?

Have they already come to Earth and not liked what they found?

Can they see that we are in a pattern of destruction and they want to help?

Are they here now, helping us?

Have they seen destruction on other planets or in other solar systems and, seeing their destruction, is there a solution to our problem that can be seen from other solar systems?

Should we learn about outer space functions to understand our way of life?

The unknown quantum leap vs. the basic concept of reality (what you don't know can't hurt you or what you do know needs correcting)

Thought Consciousness

We are all creatures of habit – I'm from Missouri the "show me" state (scientists). Prove it! If one does not understand - prove it! What one should do is use one's own mind and thoughts to except "what you don't know – won't hurt you, what you see will hurt you. If one doesn't have a belief system – beliefs transfer into thought one can travel into the soul light dream consciousness of positive energy of reality. Thought is life!

The human soul is light shimmering or moving in all kinds of directions. One must direct this light in a code of trust. One must be part of that thought into the 5th dimension. Put our mind and thoughts together as one – one can move or lift an object with their mind – unknown to how man – think one can run faster if one is frightened.

Meditates. – Learns how to breathe using one breath and a thought of soul consciousness. One's spirit is advanced an unbelievable distance.

Black Hole (5ᵗʰ Dimension) (theory)

What are words? What is the meaning of words? A simple quote of a word can change the direction of time. One's mind is simple and can cope with the harsh reality of life. The world is full of questions. How far should one go or have to go to find the solution to why one exists here on old Mother Earth? Question: Is the world coming to an end? Does one want to know? How far will one travel to understand the unknown, the mystery of life the hidden secret about the end is coming.

Let me introduce to you my theory of energy time travel and why one must get on board the soul light of consciousness positive energy reality of life. The energy flows through and around us with no sign of stopping. A continuous movement.

(Theory)

The Black Hole (a mystery). Scientists have tried to come up with a theory on how the black hole operates. An object is put in and comes out to the unknown. The flow of the magnetic energy is so strong and misunderstood. It leads one to a misguided false perception of life.

(Theory)

Dark Matter. One looks at it as a negative factor but actually it's a positive factor in a magnetic zone of dark matter and white matter energy. My theory is simple; the universe, the Heavenly Body, possibly using the negative magnetic field for balance, reverses the black hole negative energy. The white hole is positive energy. Remember, the energy never stops moving. But in what direction?

The secret code will make this possible. Why does one need a secret code? It's very simple. Because we humans are the secret code of consciousness. Mankind has held the secret code inside one for a lifetime and now one will learn how to release the soul light secret code. Just keep on breathing and each breath will form into the soul light heavenly body of a secret code of consciousness.

The Plot/The Secret (my Theory)

To advance into the heavenly body will come at a time when the pyramid's magnetic field comes in contact with the cycle of reverse black hole/dark matter and white hole/positive matter cycle of balance negative and positive soul light energy. There will be an energy force like never before. This energy force will be so strong that it will make all tornadoes, earthquakes and other destructive forces feel like a breath of fresh air. The impact will change our soul light in the direction of complete heavenly body, of peace on Earth. What a beautiful concept! And it can happen, if one believes in the soul light dream consciousness of positive energy of reality.

The Black Hole. The 5ᵗʰ Dimension.

The big question: What direction does energy flow? One is always looking up or out in space to solve or find the mystery of life, in an upward energy direction. How far is up? Until we get to the point of no return? That the energy direction forms a cycle that heavenly cycle body of life travels in a clockwise direction, to keep energy movement in balance. White Matter energy flows in a positive direction clockwise, that is when the Black Hole, negative energy comes out. Where one starts in an energy direction one will end up back where one started, in a downward cycle of energy life.

Enter into the secret to save Mother Earth – the 5ᵗʰ Dimension.

In order for this theory to operate, one must look at the Big Picture.

The ocean energy flows in what direction? The land mass must use a magnetic flow to keep the direction of the ocean's energy flow in balance. At one point the negative magnetic energy flow, Dark Matter, changes into the positive energy flow, White Matter, creating the paranormal type of Black Hole. Energy doesn't stop or disappear. Energy just travels into a new dimension of the unknown 5ᵗʰ dimension soul light consciousness energy of reality of life. We are a part of that human existence energy of life, traveling in a direction of hope, peace, love and tranquility. Our replacement is our soul. A soul is taken for granted but needs to be understood for future life expectation with the weather destruction will bring on hope, the soul light of hope of consciousness, energy travel into the reality of a better life.

(The 5th dimension is mentioned in the Bible)

Note: Some will question – what will happen with the 4th dimension? It is part if the 5 dimensions.

Reverse Engineering. (Theory)

Reverse magnetic field concept – use that data to help understand the unknown (just a theory). The theory, what you don't see, won't hurt you, what won't hurt you, you don't have to see. The understanding in the 4th – 5th dimension, we may not want to understand the dark matter (religion). But listening to the sound of the Black Hole/White Hole energy, feeling the movement, there is a Morse code. A code for one to understand from the stars. A Morse Code.

Black Hole Theory. It may drastically change the way we think about our way of life. Dark Matter, Black Hole sucks all matter in with magnetic force. White Matter, positive force, reverses this form with a negative force using Nano tech. The new object is so small that the positive white energy magnetic field only sucks in a version of the Nano chip, power force vs. negative force. Data from the Nano chip gives one 4th – 5th dimension of travel.

Second Theory – Concept/Thought

Black Hole Travel = Magnetic field control = dark matter, solid form = magnetic cycle = Nano technology time chip, recording the black hole/ dark matter, white hole matter travel without seeing it, but listening to it. What one hears with 4 to 5 dimensions will let one feel and hear travel and understand. That it is just a matter of time that one will understand the cycle of life into the heavenly body of life reality take a snapshot picture of my soul light dream consciousness of positive energy of the 5th dimension of reality.

CHAPTER 6

THE BIG CHANGE
SOUL LIGHT DREAM
(THE BIG CHANGE) THE
BIG SECRET PLOT

The way one lives on this Earth will change drastically. Age will be a factor for health reasons. Those living 70 years old and above will live in a controlled environment. Social Security income will be a thing of the past.

Class Breakdown – with the meltdown of the north and south poles the land mass will be mostly water. Human beings with advanced technology (Nano Technology) will be protected.

First Class – rich, powerful, greedy humans will live in outer space. Perhaps Mars?

Second Class will live in the mountains performing underground operations.

Robot/Mechanical will be a main factor on how first class people will live.

Third Class people will live under water (Nano Technology)

From ocean living to mountain living, travel transport will be done by robotics. The breakdown of the human workload will be given only by education. To get into college one must have a Nano Technology transplant for advanced learning. Twenty five percent of the workload on Earth will be accomplished by robots/machines programmed to do repetitive work. Fifty percent of the humans living underwater will do labor work; acquiring minerals needed for outer space. Twenty five percent of humans will live in the mountains and underground doing scientific work for outer space living and supplies.

First Class outer space humans will be controlling the second and third class humans with laser beam technology to supply their needs and lifestyle.

The four seasons – weather will no longer exist. To live comfortably one must wear protective clothing and breathing apparatuses for clean air to exist. There will be a class's outbreak to change over the two party systems but to no avail. One World order will be too strong. The super power nations (Russia, Germany, England, France) will come on board with the United States for outer space living.

<u>My Snapshot Picture of Soul Light Consciousness of Energy Reality</u>

<u>The Last Piece of the Pie – The Big Change -Nano Technology</u>

1. Ocean Living
2. Underground Living
3. Mountain Living
4. Outer Space Living
5. Planet Living
6. Alien/Human Living
7. Remove Viewing and Telepathy - Paranormal

<u>Environmental Living</u>

1. Weather Changes (disaster, oil, over flooding)
2. Earthquakes
3. Volcanoes
4. Rain
5. Land – Ocean Living

Warning – Millions of animals will die because of our disregard for life. This will be a wake-up period for one to make a change.

A snapshot picture of fear vs. nuclear weapons. Mother Nature's destruction, time is near the end, the dream will give you the secret to take away this fear. One must come under the umbrella of dream protection. If not there is no protection. One must believe this dream is a way to come together all over the world, to stop the destruction with the soul light consciousness, positive energy of reality protection.

In my dream and story, "The Last Piece of the Pie Theory" is weather, and the vast changes in weather destruction will come before the nuclear destruction, destroying all destructive weapons.

There is no protection from this deed, but if one comes together in this energy mind control, the last piece of the pie will be solved. This soul light dream will come to pass. The great protection snapshot of the soul light dream umbrella of energy reality.

The Big Change

As I mentioned in the previous chapter, I will give one a picture postcard of the direction one is headed. Good vs. Evil. Special interest groups vs. greed. Follow the money. The picture is there. Open one's eyes! One can see the picture of the big wheel turning in a way of deception and greed. See the picture of One World Order controlling masses of people? See the big picture of outer space living vs. robots as slaves? See the poor people living under water with Nano Technology? Bringing up the last supply of food existing on Earth because of the weather destruction. See the picture of humans and robots living in the innovation, demanding the supplies from the ocean, robots and humans working as slaves, these minerals are beamed up to the advanced rich people on another planet for survival, how long can this lifestyle last? It is a terrible life for human existence. Their religious faith is dwindling. The food under the ocean has come to a halt. A big change is needed.

Beautiful concept, intelligent human beings were created to enjoy this beautiful creation, but until then and until now, this beautiful way of life is being destroyed because of human greed and human frailties.

Earth is the oldest planet in our solar system. One is traveling to the other planets to learn more about how we exist now and in the future. The uncertainty of life here on Earth has been a continuous pattern until the end of time. That is why I am writing this book through my dream state of mind with my soul light dream understanding. My soul light connection is supplying me with this information. If I am wrong or right there will be a continuous soul light contacting other human beings with a solution to save old Mother Earth. Look for other books or look at the person next to you. Just remember one thing – THE WEATHER IS CHANGING! Look out! Be prepared! Get in touch with your soul/spirit consciousness. One needs to travel in the energy direction of reality.

Earth is the answer to higher life and living. Understand old Mother Earth and one will be at peace.

Decisions – The Three Big Tests

Because of the global melt down (warming), the unpredictable vast weather changes and the future outlook, it is almost impossible for Earth to survive another disaster. For years the elite societies all over the world have built space ships to travel to other planets. Only the people with power and money will be chosen to leave old Mother Earth. This will involve millions of families. There will be a lot of resentment and angry people fighting to get on board but to no avail. There will be two more choices. Second choice is to travel to outer space with the advanced aliens living with humans here on Earth. This movement will also be a difficult task to accomplish. A lot of people will have been destroyed before the aliens took control. The aliens will only want the educated middle class people. All that will be left on Earth will be millions of poor, sick and hopeless people. But the hopelessness will not last long. The space ship called Crystal Ball Ship of Life will be there to enable all those left behind to get on board, destination unknown, to return to old Mother Earth upon the completion of the big disaster.

NEW WORLD

Alternative universe – the cycle of life ship goes into the universe – hold one in a suspended state of mind. One's thought – one's concept – two or more reality - vision – out there – two realities as one using quantum physics will advance energy into the fifth dimension. The soul consciousness must be involved. The brain can only feel what one's soul light energy observes.

Sounds: Hear, feel, thought of consciousness of positive energy will be a new energy travel of reality.

We have just recently learned that oil and gas are not biological – a myth. Bi antic= oil. Gas is naturally located all over the world. This information was kept a secret because of greed and power (follow the money).

Have you ever looked at patterns on the wall, and if you ever look long enough, you see a picture form of life. A message. Look at the stars long enough and you will see the fifth dimension energy code. The puzzle, the picture, is worth a thousand words.

My seven soul light dream of reality theory, the fifth dimension. What is the truth/ the spirit/ the soul meditation? Use the left side of the brain = spirit/soul light spirit. One thought, one thought energy part of the energy travel into my soul light dream. The stars in the solar system are part of the code to the fifth dimensions stardust energy. Crystal Ball Energy = peace on old Mother Earth.

THE BIG CHANGE

Outer space people will be known as the lost race of people. The runaways. The advanced people lost contact with the Earth people over a period of time. The last beam up of products was lost in space. There is also no more communication. The last living sound will be a beep, lingering on for years but with no location or response.

The return of the lost people, with their technology advanced for hundreds of years, will look upon us as aliens when they return to Earth. They will not look like the Earth people as before, with no color or change of color by climate. What goes around comes around.

CHAPTER 7

THE NEW WORLD POWER OF LIFE REALITY ISRAEL / AFRICA

The end and the beginning. The New Beginning. Africa will be the place where the New World Power of Life Reality will appear, one start, one location, and one soul light of human consciousness of reality. One color, one race for all human beings, but one can change when traveling in the direction of other countries. For example, one is black when entering another country. One language – telepathy. The mystery of the basic concept of race is that one can never stay one color. Color will change with the climate and because of location. For example, when one travels into another country, one will be that color and speak that language by telepathy. We are all one being, one soul light, to live in harmony and solitude. The color of one human being will not determine one's fate or power over another human being.

Africa is the largest continent and, at one time had all the resources. It was the richest of all the continents. But now Africa is looked upon as a lost civilization by most countries. Africa is not a threat to any country, for example – Israel. History comes from Africa. Now looking for their own country, Israel will need Africa for support. In the future coming years, Africa will be the country that will have a rebirth into a productive, unknown richness. Such a powerful force that all countries will use Africa as an example to change their lifestyle. Step by step, education, home schooling, and scientific development to the highest invention, unlimited advancement and resources.

Aliens living in Africa.

Aliens have tried to live in other countries but to no avail because of their looks, color and even because of their higher intellect. They would not get along with authority. Aliens migrated to Africa, not because of their poor way of life but because they saw the new, reborn advancement. Africa is looked upon as a stupid, poor, helpless continent, but with the new found crystal ball there will be a New Beginning crystal ball equal to an unknown substance that the world has never seen. With the vast wealth changes in other countries, the new beginning will start over in Africa form the rebirth way of living is in my dream world. One's energy soul light dream lives – not acts. New way of spiritual way of life. Soul light, the sun, the energy, the rebirth of life's basic way of life with a new advanced technology. A village of love and understanding. It is coming! In Africa with the land mass changes. Africa – my soul light dream consciousness of reality existence.

First there will be a warning – let me make one thing clear – there is no other destructive power on Earth from all of the nuclear power countries can destroy these crystal balls, the heart of the crystal ball will come in all shapes, forms and sizes. They will move and travel in mysterious ways, undetected. There will be non-believers who will try to use force but to no avail, countless people will die but the outcome will be victorious. It's time! Time for the new beginning! The Big Change! The human race with power is out of control. Never again. Never again. If you don't understand go back in history. It hasn't been that long but we sometimes choose to forget. Get on board with my soul light dream consciousness of reality.

The New Advanced Movement of Africa / Israel

The reason I chose Africa / Israel as the last piece of the pie is that I know and feel deep down in my heart that a big change in this world, old Mother Earth, needs to come <u>now</u>, not tomorrow or sometime in the future. It is now, all Israel is asking for is the last piece of the pie. A place to call home, a country, a place to live in peace and tranquility and to share the last piece of the pie. If the weather changes do not change the land mass and the situation remains the same – with fear, hate and possible destruction – then my soul light dream consciousness of positive energy of reality, my soul light dream, will introduce the pyramid in Israel and pyramid in Africa. A crystal ball with energy forces so great that all nations will fall to their knees and surrender to the crystal ball's power. This power will last until there is a complete turnaround of peace on Earth and goodwill to all mankind. (NEVER AGAIN).

Winter. The New Beginning.

The reason I chose winter first is that is where it will start, the climate, the weather, Alaska and the North Pole, if the United States is used as an example. This will apply to all the other countries here on Earth. It will be a worldwide chain of events.

This chain of events will move fast, weather and destruction, mainly because one has read or talked about or has seen these winter changes now and in the past.

I am given a picture postcard of the big weather changes. Through the eyes of the soul light consciousness energy of reality movement. One postcard. It is nighttime in a cold dreary time (atmosphere?). The darkness remains for a period of time without the concept of time. When that has ended, light will slowly creep into the existing darkness. The winter at the North Pole and South Pole is not the same. There is dry land that has emerged from under the water forming a picture of a heavenly soul light. The soul light being cannot be readily identified but the picture of life is there. The thought, question – what's happening? The reality – a new direction of living on old Mother Earth in a soul light consciousness energy of reality. Live a vision. A concept. A spirit of life existence.

Spring. The New Beginning.

Far out there is a land of twenty different islands. A picture of darkness came upon these islands; the darkness remained for a long period of time. In fact, there was no time. The weather changes were unbelievable and the picture of soul light changed. There was beauty. The twenty islands had come together as one. One soul light consciousness of energy and reality into a heavenly body of existence.

Summer. The New Beginning.

The continent of Africa, the largest continent on old Mother Earth, is in darkness. The picture is the same. The picture of darkness remaining for a long period of soul light time. No one ever realized that there was time. And then there was light. The light came slowly with a view. There were not words to express the beauty of the soul light existence in Africa. This new Africa will be the center point on how the rest of the countries will live and operate in to the soul light consciousness of reality, what a picture! In order for one to see this picture they have to go on to the next step. There will be pyramids in every country on old Mother Earth. These pyramids will be looked upon as a guiding star in the fourth and fifth dimensions, to open the door as a guide into the heavenly body of everlasting thought, spirit of soul reality of life.

Fall. The New Beginning.

The fall pattern is the most unique pattern of all. The fall did not have a long period of darkness; the fall was the positive way of soul light consciousness energy of reality of life. The fall is when the sunlight rose and shone upon Mother Earth in a mysterious warm way of light that is everything that the sun encompassed was made whole. It was like a new beginning, in the seven-soul light consciousness energy of reality dream. This dream was introduced to all mankind. No one was exempted.

The Secret Code.

"We are all just a piece of the pie"

Do you really want to know what the secret of the last piece of the pie is? Okay. I will tell you, but don't get too worked up over the surprise. Will the last piece of the pie give one hope for the future? Will it make one a better person? Will it help one to love and respect one another? Is the hatred so strong that it is irreversible? Hate equals love equals openness to the soul light consciousness of energy of life reality. That last piece of the pie is for all. It is big enough to feed everyone, but only a few can partake of this wondrous concept of life reality. Why? If one can accept and feel the code of least resistance, the dream state of soul light consciousness existence, one can move on into the winter, spring, summer and fall. Yes, know the present, past and future and most of all, travel into the heavenly body of everlasting solitude of one mind, spirit and peace of mind. It is that simple. No hard work, just be prepared. Open up! One mind to the soul light consciousness energy of life reality. No, that's not the way to have the last piece of the pie. When one realizes that there may be just one piece of the pie that can sustain one into the future of life reality, there is hope. Hope that one will be around for the last piece of the pie. Hope and understanding that one and all are connected to and make up and depend on each other to understand the connection of one soul consciousness that will give one hope. Without hope one cannot exist into the life of reality. And now, the rest of the story.

Dwindal Toliver's Grandmother

CHAPTER 8

THE CRYSTAL BALL POWER WOMEN/MOTHERS * * * OUT OF THE PYRAMID IN AFRICA * * *

The Last Piece of the Pie

The Big Surprise Ending. I never had a mother or father to put their arms around me and say, "I love you".

What is life? When did it all begin? How was life created? One can go back in history for the answers and one will have been introduced to the mystery of life. I am happy to experience this wonder of living on old Mother Earth of reality.

Mother Earth rings a profound bell in my ear. I didn't know my mother or father when I was a little child. My grandmother was my mother and father all in one bundle of joy. Precious memories, how they linger in my soul, even today. It is hard for me to express how I truly feel deep down in my soul. The beautiful thought process that is going through my heart and mind at this time. How I feel and missed the love of not having a mother and father. I miss the understanding of my grandmother's love.

I love football and baseball. I had entertained the thought of playing football or baseball but missed the opportunity of playing because of my military commitment. At this time I am associated with five outstanding men that I have had the opportunity of playing WITH in a football pool in my old age. This is my joy, my piece of mind and love. I love having these friends in my life. The big enjoyment that I get out of the football pool, besides winning the pool most of the time, is watching the football players acknowledge their mothers and God when they are interviewed on the TV camera. It brings tears to my eyes and I think about my grandmother and the unselfish, unconditional love she bestowed on me. And now I'm thinking about the millions of mothers all over the world who gave life to a baby soul to live and to experience the joy and downfalls of living on old Mother Earth. I am blessed and I feel the need to end my book, <u>The Last Piece of the Pie</u> with my seven soul light dreams of consciousness of positive energy and reality. I don't think that there could be a better end than to recognize and give praise to all of the mothers living here on old Mother Earth. It's time! Recognition is now! My soul light dream is a tool to bring all positive energy mothers together. Open one's mind and heart and give praise to the Almighty! Know that without our mothers, the soul light dream consciousness of positive energy of reality, we would not be here to enjoy life. I want to go a step further. Women outnumber men by a ratio of eight to one but do not have the equal rights of a man. This must change and it will change if all of you beautiful mothers get on board the soul light dream consciousness of positive energy of reality!

You are My last piece of the pie! Without you old Mother Earth would be an empty shell of life reality. Do this for me. Make my soul light dream come true. Be president of the United States of America or be what you are, but be great at it and bring old Mother Earth to a balance of life reality like we've never seen before! I have tears in my eyes and love in my heart when writing this chapter "A New Beginning", for the crystal ball power for the women and mothers of life reality.

Introduction of the crystal ball power of life reality will come in all shapes and forms. These crystal ball powers will travel so fast, in the blink of an eye. It's there! Picture being at a sporting event with millions of people and this humming sound from the crystal ball power appears in the sky in a cloud formation. The humming sound is so great that people will fall to their knees - and then there is no sound. Millions of crystal ball power flakes fall down from above like snowflakes. These crystal ball power flakes will enter only women and mothers, unknowingly, all over the world. The crystal ball power energy will come from the pyramid in Africa.

Crystal Ball Mystery Strength

❖ Mysteries are yet to be discovered and, because its mystical powers are given to women and mothers, follow the pyramid location. Follow the birth of a baby girl. Follow the direction of women. Listen to the mother giving birth.
❖ The crystal ball power will be like a bouncing ball form of light.

Now you see it, now you don't. You may see it, feel it, as a sign of an unbelievable sound. Strength! The source of the unknown crystal energy power is just what it is perceived to be. Unknown. This will be given to all of the women and mothers of this world. The outcome from this mysterious, mystical power is also unknown to women and mothers. They will know how to use this power when it is needed. It will never be misused. If it is used for one's own power, one will be destroyed.

❖ You are that blind fate of justice. My soul light dream consciousness of positive energy of reality would like to celebrate some of the outstanding accomplishments of women and mothers. I don't want to mention names because there are so many, just the fields that women are in and that they are the top of the mark:

• Actress
• Madam/Secretary
• Queen
• FBI/CIA agent
• Military General
• Chancellor

The list could go on and on but, because of the "good old boys" network, women are shut out of the upper echelon of power. Your rights as a mother are slowly taken away. Women, you need to march on Washington D.C. by the millions, voicing your opinions and shouting "I'm mad and I won't take it anymore!" It's time! It's time to use your crystal ball power and knowledge to make the change. To save old Mother Earth! To be that New Beginning! And above all, pave the way for the children to have a better future in life. Teach your children to be leaders, not followers.

Secret Code (Bring peace to everyone with Crystal Ball Power)

❖ Soul light dream mothers and women, you are the resume of life experiences.

❖ You are the puzzle of positive energy that will keep the weather in balance – winter/spring/summer/fall.

❖ You are the big wheel of positive energy life that will help keep the big wheel spinning into the heavenly body of life reality.

❖ You are the stars energy that will cycle the rainbow in the direction of the crystal ball of energy power that will bring peace to old Mother Earth.

❖ You are the soul light positive energy force that will help control the earthquakes, volcanoes, global warming and take old Mother Earth into the fifth dimension reality of life.

❖ You are the soul light that will help bring stem cells and the Nano Technological revolution.

❖ You are the religious spirit energy force that will help to bring peace to all mankind, for others to follow and be as one, positive energy.

❖ Above all, women and mothers, you are my soul light dream of thought, intuition, vision, wisdom and creativity. My pledge is that you are my dream state of openness into the last piece of the pie. A snapshot picture of my soul light dream consciousness of positive energy of reality.

Mothers you have the built in intuition to make a change, a positive energy change, to bring one love, peace and happiness to old Mother Earth.

❖ Mother, you are the rainbow of life.

❖ Mother, you are the bright star that will bring us into the fifth dimension.

❖ Mother, you are the change that will make a difference in our government policies.

❖ Mother, you are the advanced technology of the future.

❖ Mother, you are the negative/positive energy that flows into

❖ the heavenly body of peace.

❖ Mother, you are the crystal ball of power to make the Big
❖ Change.
❖ Mother, you are our religious hope.
❖ Mother, above all, you are the snapshot picture of my soul light dream consciousness of positive energy of reality.

My pledge is for you and for others to follow their hearts with thought, vision, creativity, soul/spirit and love. Make old Mother Earth proud of your accomplishments! <u>PEACE.</u>

POEM THE PERFECT ROSE (TO ALL THE WOMEN/MOTHERS)

- You are so Special
- A rose is but a rose – like a picture that is worth a thousand words.
- Woman/mother you are that rose and that picture that has played its part, the puzzle that needs to be solved.
- So let's combine our positive energy and be as one. For the crystal ball power of women/mothers on this earth.
- And now it's time
- The secret code is out
- Women/Mothers are the ones.
- The crystal ball power that you possess – It's time for you to make old mother earth proud of you.

Oh how special you are to have given birth to all mankind. Without you women/mothers we are nothing – you have that unique set of abilities to bring or give birth is the highest honor that one can possess.

THE LAST PIECE OF THE PIE RESUME

Old Mother Earth, you are special!

You are my mystery lade, with rank and authority!

You are my soul light dream consciousness of positive energy of reality!

You are my puzzling strength of something not understood, but believed. Old Mother Earth.

You are my quality, my interpretation of life here and after.

You are my mysterious-ness way of life along with beauty and when you shine it is like a new beginning.

You are a mystical, spiritual way of life that promotes harmony.

You mystify with myth and everlasting strength and belief, thanks for the last piece of the pie on Old Mother Earth.

Old Mother Earth, you are special and, above all, you are that woman / mother crystal ball power of life reality!

You have sustained life in all shapes and forms.

I am proud to have been a part of its existence of life reality.

Old Mother Earth, you are my cycle of life that brings love and happiness.

You are my amazing grace, "How sweet the sound"!

Old Mother Earth, the big source of power that you possess, the true wonders of positive energy that moves in a mysterious way, have given one hope for a better life!

Old Mother Earth, you were given the birth of life, for all to enjoy. The everlasting soul light consciousness of positive energy of life reality.

Thanks for letting me be a little bit part of me in you!

THE LAST PIECE OF THE PIE

If I had the authority to choose my soul light president – present or in the soul light hereafter would be former President Jimmy Carter.

He is one of the most compassionate individuals I have ever known or heard of. Jimmy Carter is constantly helping the Third World countries. He is a great leader among great leaders I am dedicating my book to Jimmy Carter and his wife, Roselyn, hoping that other Presidents will follow in his footsteps, working toward peace and tranquility in the Third World countries and here in this country.

CHAPTER 10

ORIGINAL WORKS OF ART BY DWINDAL TOLIVER

a Last Salute to the President
John F. Kennedy Jr.

Staying Healthy

Earvin Magit Johnso

DC Goliver

Printed in the United States
By Bookmasters